THE HOUSE THAT JACK'S FRIENDS BUILT

Written by Gare Thompson

Illustrated by Winifred Barnum-Newman

STECK-VAUGHN
ELEMENTARY · SECONDARY · ADULT · LIBRARY

A Harcourt Classroom Education Company

www.steck-vaughn.com

Young Jack didn't have a house of his own.

He wanted to build one, but couldn't alone.

So he called on his friends and said with a grin,

"Will you help build my house? It's time to begin."

One friend that helped was Paul.

All by himself, he put up each wall.

Paul was so careful with every brick.

The walls he built were strong and thick.

4

Along came Ellie, right through the door.

She helped put down a brand new floor.

Jack and Ellie worked through the night.

Then they shined it up, all clean and bright.

Another friend came whose name was Lynn.

She helped Jack build a roof of tin.

They worked and worked and did not stop,

Until the chimney was placed on top.

Jack needed more help right away,

So he called on his best friend, Jay.

They built a kitchen, bedroom, and den,

Plus a dining room that seated ten.

Just a few things were left to do,

So Jack got a front door and painted it blue.

The final touch was a welcome mat.

Then in he moved with his dog and cat.

Now Jack had the finest house in town.

He stretched and sighed as he sat down.

He fell asleep and dreamed of each friend,

Who worked and worked until the end.

Then Jack knew what he had to do.

He called on his pals and said, "I need you!"

I can't live here without you, too.

So they all lived together...what a crew!